Meet Me Under The Mistletoe

Tammy Dennings Maggy

Dedication

The inspiration for this story came from the bond I share with my husband, Liam. From the moment we met, I knew he was my one and only. My journey to find him wasn't an easy one. Filled with heartache and pain, I nearly gave up. Then he was just there. He built me up and let me find myself again. He let me fly always knowing I'd return back to the safety of his arms again. I love you, mo anam cara.

He'd spent twenty years in the Coast Guard and has since retired with honor from his service but at the time I wrote this story he was active duty. Early in our marriage I faced the distinct possibility he'd have to be "underway" for over three hundred days out of the year. Fortunately, he didn't have to go, but many of our friends had to go and be separated from their loved ones. Many missed births, first steps, first words and yet still these brave men and women fulfill their duty.

To me, Steve and Jolene in **Meet Me Under the Mistletoe** represent all those Coast Guard families who've sacrificed their time together to keep the rest of us safe. For all you do, from the bottom of my heart— I thank you.

Semper Paratus.

CONTENTS

CHAPTER 1

December 22nd, Present Day US Coast Guard Air Station
Cold Bay, Alaska

"Pon pon, pon pon, pon pon, this is COMSTA Kodiak. An unknown distress call was received on channel 16 FM. All mariners transiting the area are requested to keep a sharp lookout and report all sightings to this or any Coast Guard station. This is COMSTA Kodiak, out."

Petty Officer Steve Sanders grabbed his gear from the ready station to check through it once again. His gut told him this wasn't going to be an average day for the crab fleet. Starting in the middle of the night, the US Coast Guard Communication Station in Kodiak picked up multiple calls from vessels throughout the King Crab fishing grounds. Up until now, none had sent out a distress call, but with another storm building up strength over the Bering Sea, it was only a matter of time before his unit would be sent into action.

Glancing over his shoulder at the teddy bear dressed in a Coast Guard swimmer wet suit, he smiled. In less than a month, he'd be a father and his team never let a day go by without reminding him. Once he found a pack of diapers along with his own "survival kit" complete with nose plugs, tongs and thick rubber gloves stuffed in his locker. Another instance it was a box of chocolate cigars, half with pink wrappers and the other with blue. The day before he left for his current three-month stint in Cold Bay, his unit on Kodiak threw a couples' baby shower for him and his wife Jolene. The teddy bear was a gift from the Commander, and Jolene made sure to pack it in his duffel when he wasn't looking. It was simply her way of reminding him to come home safe for her and their child.

A handwritten gift tag dangled from a red velvet ribbon tied around the bear's neck. It read, *"Meet me under the mistletoe and I'll make all your Christmas wishes come true."* Every single year since he was a fifteen year-old freshman in high school and he dared a then thirteen year-old Jolene to meet him under the mistletoe, they'd never missed a chance to get that first holiday kiss. Of course, if the fiery brunette would've punched him instead of kissed him that first time, who knows where his life would be now?

That first kiss began an annual tradition neither of them ever dreamed of breaking. To them it meant as much as their wedding vows during their handfasting ceremony on Christmas Eve. At the stroke of midnight, they had been pronounced spouses for life under a large bouquet of mistletoe of course. Now here he was only three short days before another anniversary with his soul mate and expecting their first child. Life couldn't get much better than that.

The SAR alarm sounded off, piercing his quiet moments of reflection. His heartbeat quickened as the adrenaline surged through his body. *It's go time!* The rest of his search and rescue team hustled as details of the emergency sounded over the address system.

"Fishing vessel *Northern Star* has sent out a mayday. Vessel is taking on water. Eight crew members in survival suits boarding two life rafts. Last known position twenty-five nautical miles east of St. Matthew Island. Repeat. Fishing vessel *Northern Star* listing and taking on water. Crew evacuating into life boats."

He slung his equipment bags over both shoulders and jogged toward the waiting helo. If luck was on their side, the impending storm would hold back a bit longer and the rescue should go off without a hitch. However, the Bering Sea had a life of its own, and at any moment their luck could change on a dime. As part of his routine on each mission, he bowed his head in prayer. *Goddess, I ask you help us find these sailors and bring them home safe. Please hold back the waves until all are safe aboard with us and headed home.*

* * * *

December 22nd, Present Day Kodiak Island, Alaska

Jolene turned up the emergency radio to hear the distress call. As the wife of a Coast Guard rescue swimmer, she had picked up the habit of keeping her radio always tuned to channel 16 whenever her husband was on duty during crab fishing season. It was her way of keeping track of him and the fisherman she'd come to consider part of her family.

"Mayday, mayday, mayday. This is the *Northern Star*. Rogue wave hit disabling the vessel. Engine room taking on water. Sinking fast. All eight are abandoning ship into life rafts. We've lost all power. Last known position nearly thirty nautical miles east of St. Matthew. Repeat. Mayday, mayday, mayday. *Northern Star* is taking on water. Entire crew is heading for life rafts. All in survival suits."

Her stomach clenched. She knew the wives of five of the fisherman on that boat. Two of them worked with her at the hospital. As one of the few registered nurses on the island, Jolene knew all the local families. Any kind of emergency brought them all together and it looked like today was going to be a doozy. *Better get rolling. No point in trying to go back to sleep. Might as well head in and start my shift early.*

She tossed the covers back and slowly slid her swollen feet into her fuzzy slippers. There was no way she'd walk barefooted over the freezing hard wood floors this time of year. Although at eight and a half months pregnant, the cold often felt good when they were as swollen as they were at the moment. She stopped her shuffle to the bathroom and slipped her right foot out of the slipper and onto the floor. The chill radiated up from the floor, taking her breath away, and that was before her sole even made contact. She shoved her foot back into the warm slipper and continued on with her morning routine.

The hot water of the shower worked out all the kinks in her back as she ran the washcloth over her ever-expanding belly. "Well, little one. Your daddy is heading out on another day to save lives. Don't you worry, though. He'll be here for our kiss under the mistletoe. This same time next year, you'll be joining us there, but this time you'll just have to settle for kicking him through my belly."

In response, she watched as a little foot made its way across her stretched skin and gave her another kick. She smiled as tears rolled down her cheeks. These were the things Steve missed out on when he was underway. It'd taken them nearly ten years to finally get pregnant, and now she had to experience all the little things alone. Keeping a detailed baby journal helped her husband stay in the loop as did their Skype calls, but somehow it wasn't the same.

Six other times she'd managed to conceive, only to have their excitement dashed a few months later with miscarriages. This pregnancy was the only one nearly to term and so far everything had gone without a hitch—for the baby that is. Jolene suffered from debilitating morning sickness for her entire first trimester leaving her on bed rest for most of it. Two weeks ago her doctor dropped another bomb. She had gestational diabetes. It wasn't unexpected, but just one more thing to add to the list of issues she had to go through alone.

As the steamy water continued to work on her muscles, she remembered the weekend they conceived their baby. Steve surprised her in the middle of her shift at the hospital with a dozen pale purple roses. He had won the lottery in his unit and gotten an extra two days of liberty. Lucky for her, the other nurses had been more than willing to cover the remainder of her shift.

As soon as they'd made it through the door of their condo, he had tossed her over his shoulder and bolted toward the bedroom. "I'm going to taste every inch of your body until you beg for mercy."

* * * *

CHAPTER 2

April 22nd, Eight months ago Kodiak Island, Alaska

Steve's hand slapped her ass one, twice, then three times. "Stop squirming, woman. I mean to have you naked and quivering all weekend."

She bit her lower lip to prevent from crying out. Her husband knew exactly how to get her wet and ready to be ravished in seconds. She wanted nothing more than to be dominated by him twenty-four hours a day. Before his last assignment, they'd explored more of their fantasies including spanking. He had perfected his technique of the fast openhanded slap, sudden and sharp enough to make the loud cracking sound, but hard enough only to sting and make her ass a warm rosy color.

"Put me down and let me get out of these scrubs first. I've been on my feet for over eighteen hours and can't smell very good."

He tossed her onto the bed and pinned her there, arms above her head. His lips brushed over hers sending a jolt of electricity slamming through her body. "Mmm...you smell fucking fantastic to me, Jo. I need you now. Three months away from you and your body has been sheer torture."

She lifted her head so their lips touched and slipped her tongue over his until he moaned. "It's been hell without you, too, babe, but how about we move this homecoming party to the bathroom? You know how much I love to be fucked in the shower."

He smiled the slow sexy grin that had captured her heart when they were kids. "Now you're talking." He kicked off his boots and sat up. Still straddling her body, he lifted his shirt up over his head while she worked to relieve him of his belt.

Her fingertips grazed over his ripped abdominal muscles and up his chest as he lowered his body back on top of hers. After kicking her shoes off, she wrapped her legs around his waist and her arms around his neck as his lips crushed hers, demanding and possessive.

He backed off the bed with her wrapped around his body. His arms held her tight against his chest as their tongues continued to slip and slide over each other. He kicked open the partially closed bathroom door as his fingers worked at the clasp of her bra under her scrub top.

She broke the kiss only long enough to lift her shirt over her head.

He pinned her back against the door and scooped both of her tits into his hands. He popped first one nipple and then the other into his mouth as he firmly kneaded each fleshy mound. "Mine."

"Yes, baby. All yours." Her fingers ran through his sandy blond hair as he sucked harder and harder, bringing both of her nipples to painful erections. She unwrapped her legs from around his waist as he held her up until her feet touched the floor. She reached between them to find the zipper. Her hands slipped under the waistband and shoved his pants and briefs down over his taut ass.

His jaw clenched and unclenched as her fingers dug into his flesh. "Damn, girl. You know what that does to me."

"Uh huh." She moved her hands from his ass, over his hips, and back between them to find his cock bouncing with need. Her fingers wrapped around his hard, throbbing shaft and squeezed as she stroked him. "And what does that do for you?"

"On fire. I want to bury it into your hot tight pussy, but we need to do something about these scrub bottoms." His fingers jerked open the tie at her waist and shoved his right hand down the front to cup her shaved outer lips. Two fingers slipped through and into her.

"God, yes." Her voice faltered as his thumb brushed against her swollen clit. She shoved her pants further down her legs until they dropped to the floor.

He removed his fingers from inside her and noisily sucked them. "Nothing tastes sweeter than you when you're hot and horny." He stepped out of his pants and tore off his socks.

She reached behind her to turn on the shower only seconds before he caught her up in his arms again. Standing over six inches taller than her five and a half foot frame, he always had to lift her up to keep them face to face. Not that she minded one bit. It was where she felt the safest, free to let just let go and submit completely to his every wish and desire.

He moved them into the two-person shower without breaking eye contact. His dark brown eyes appeared black in an instant, sending shivers up and down her spine. She held his gaze as he pushed her back against the tile and spread her legs wide. A moment later his cock slid into her already dripping cunt.

* * * *

He moaned as her inner muscles clenched around his cock, pulling him in deeper. He held still for only a moment before his need to take her consumed him. He pulled out and slammed into her over and over again, her body shaking and convulsing in his arms with each stroke.

"Steve...I...don't stop. Fuck me harder!" Her husky pleas echoed off the walls amping him up even more. She raked her nails down his back as her body clenched through a powerful orgasm.

"Open your eyes, Jo. I need you to look at me."

She did as he asked. Her hazel eyes positively glowed in the dim light of the room. Her pupils dilated even further and pulled him in.

This moment he craved every second they've been apart from each other. The connection between them deepened beyond physical at that instant and he finally allowed himself to let go completely. His orgasm slammed through his body as he exploded deep inside her. Even though his knees nearly buckled from the intensity of it, he kept pumping into her, filling her with his seed.

He rested his forehead against hers as their breathing slowed and the hot water rained down upon their flushed bodies. "God, I missed you."

She brushed her hair off her forehead as he placed her down on her feet. She settled her back against his chest, her head under his chin. "I can tell."

He kissed her forehead and reached for the shampoo. He loved to wash her hair while she clung to his body after sex. Caring for her like this made him feel just a little less guilty for leaving her alone for a month or more at a time.

She reached around and rested both her hands on his thighs as he lathered her hair. "You sure know how to treat a gal. I may just have to marry you one day."

He chuckled. "You say that every time I come home on leave. Am I away so long you forget we're already married?"

"Babe, you fuck my brains out the instant we walk in the door. I can barely remember my name let alone we've been married for nearly two decades. Being with you, like this, brings it all back to me. There's a reason people say their minds go blank during an orgasm and you give me several each time we're together."

He turned her so her hair could be under the still hot water cascade. "You do the same for me. Every single time. It gets harder and harder to leave you when I have to be on duty."

She tipped her head back out of the water and placed her hands on either side of his face. "It tears me up, too, but this is the life both of us signed up for when you joined the Coast Guard. I knew what I was getting myself into and I don't have any regrets."

"None?" His heart ached with the memory of the last miscarriage. She had to be hospitalized for nearly a week afterward. He was out on a search and rescue and didn't get word until after she'd been admitted for over three days. As soon as they returned to base, the chaplain was there to drive him straight to the hospital. She'd looked so pale in the bed propped up on at least three fluffy pillows. He thought he'd lost her until she opened her eyes and held out her arms for him to join her in the bed. Together they mourned the child they longed to hold in their arms.

"Not a one. You have to stop blaming yourself for being away doing what you need to do to save lives. No matter where you are, I can feel you with me always. The times apart make our reunions oh so much sweeter."

He softly kissed her. "That they do, darlin'." He reached for the scrunchy and loaded it up with her favorite jasmine body wash before running it all over her back and ass. He loved the feel of her skin all slick with soap under his fingers and sliding against his body. He handed her the soapy sponge while he worked the lather over her tits with both of his hands, kneading and squeezing the nipples until they firmed up once again.

Her small hands traced over his muscles, covering his skin with the sweet smelling suds. The jasmine always relaxed him and allowed the tension from work to flow down the drain with the extra soap. "How about we get out of here before the hot water runs out and we turn into two prunes? There's more I want to do to this magnificent body of yours and I don't want to rush. How long do we have this time?"

He quickly rinsed his body before shutting off the water. "Four full days before I have to catch a flight back to Cold Bay."

She stepped into the towel he held out for her and wrapped it around her body. "Well, let's make each moment count. I've got some fruit and cheeses in the fridge. Let me grab that and a bottle of wine. You set up the candles and the video camera." She wiggled her eyebrows up and down before making her way to the kitchen.

"Hot damn!"

* * * *

CHAPTER 3

December 22nd, Present Day Bering Sea, East of St. Matthew Island, Alaska

The lone raft rose and crashed with each wave. Steve studied the pattern of the wave crests and determined he had to be lowered within the next five minutes in order to get down and start sending survivors up before the next series of waves collided into them.

Down he went and dropped within three feet of the raft opening. As soon as he determined the number of survivors, the helo would send down the basket to begin the rescue. Even though his body was covered in the protective wet suit, the icy water and wind cooled his skin as soon as he broke the surface and made for the raft. Within five strokes he reached the target and grasped the outstretched hands to lift him inside.

"Man, are we happy to see you, Steve. It's been a hell of a ride out here."

He shook the survivor's hand and immediately recognized him as one of his neighbors. "Jake? When did you end up on the *Northern Star?*" He quickly ran his hands over him. "Are any of you injured?"

Jake shook his head. "We're all fine in here. Captain got us all in our suits before we jumped into the rafts. I just started with the crew last week after their first offload. Sure as hell didn't expect this when I signed up."

"What about the other raft? When was the last time you had it in sight?" Steve signaled up to the spotter to drop the basket for four survivors, no injuries.

"Haven't seen them for over an hour now. A huge wave washed over us and snapped the rope we'd secured between the rafts. One minute they were there and the next gone without a trace. We tried to raise them on the radio, but all we got was static until you guys showed up."

Steve smiled. "Good call grabbing the water proof transistors. As soon as the helo got close enough, we picked up your transmissions. It helped us pinpoint your location."

One of the other crewmembers nodded and handed the radio over. "Captain made us run through drills all the time to be sure everything became second nature to us if we had to abandon ship. God, I hope the guys in the other raft made it. I ain't never seen a wave flip a raft around like that. You could hear the rope crack as it snapped. Sounded like a gun shot."

Steve nodded and kept his face neutral as he relayed the information up to the pilot in the helo using the fishermen's transistor. The longer they stayed out there, the greater chance for a wave to flip the raft they were in, too. "Come on, let's get this show on the road. Jake, you're up first for the basket."

He held it next to the raft as Jake climbed in. After securing his friend inside the basket, he let it go and gave the signal to raise him up. Over and over again he repeated the process until all four crewmembers were aboard. Now the hard part. Steve had to stay behind with the raft until the rescue aircraft returned for him. With only enough room for the four-man crew plus three survivors, protocol dictated the swimmer was to be left behind.

He looked around at the choppy sea, tapped the top of his head and gave the thumbs up signal. Using the radio once again, he let his team know they could leave. "Go ahead. All secure here. Will await pick up."

"Roger that, swimmer. Second helo is twenty minutes out. They'll pick you up and bring you back to base."

"Copy. Swimmer out."

He watched as the helicopter turned, passing one more time over the raft before heading back to Cold Bay. From there, the survivors would be checked over by the medics on staff and then put on the next six hour flight back home to Kodiak.

He sighed and settled back against the side of the raft closest to the opening and thought of his own trip back to the island and Jolene. *Only a few more days and I'll be able to wrap my arms around her and hold on tight.* He exhaled and slowly rubbed his eyes, his body suddenly bone weary. *I'm getting too old for this shit. Maybe it's time for me to start thinking about retiring.*

* * * *

December 22nd, Present Day Kodiak Island

Jolene waddled down the hallway with a cart overflowing with Christmas decorations. She'd just finished meeting with the wives of the *Northern Star* crew. Together they decided to keep themselves occupied by decorating the children's ward for the holidays. Keeping busy was the only thing any of them could do during a time like this. No good worrying until they knew more information, but something nagged at the back of her mind ever since she heard the mayday come over the radio.

She could always tell when Steve wasn't himself, or feeling off. He had the same connection with her. In fact, he suffered right along with her during the three months of debilitating morning sickness. That part hadn't been easy for him. He had been taken off duty until his nausea could be controlled. The team couldn't have one of their most experienced rescue swimmers vomiting at the drop of a hat.

This particular rescue mission had her on edge. It was more than worrying about her friends. A cold fear threatened to take over her every thought. Maybe it was the pregnancy hormones, but she couldn't shake the thought Steve was in mortal danger.

She ducked into the bathroom, locked the door and sank to the floor in tears. She wanted to stay strong for the others, but she couldn't find the strength to do it. *Goddess of the Sea, please wrap your arms around Steve and bring him back home safe to our baby and me. I agreed to let him be with you for as long as you need him and you promised to always return him safe and sound. I'm asking— no, begging you to please keep your promise. I can't do this without him.*

A sharp knock on the door startled her out of her mini meltdown. She quickly wiped her eyes and eased herself back up to her feet. "I'll be out in a minute."

"Jo? Are you okay?"

She recognized the voice of her best friend, Madison Rivers. The only other person she'd ever allow to see her break down this way. She turned the lock and stepped back as her friend slipped inside.

Madison relocked the door and rushed to hug her. "You looked a bit pale during the meeting, hon. Is it the baby?"

She let the tears fall freely again and buried her head against her friend's shoulder. "No. It's Steve. Something's not right. I think he's in trouble. I can't shake this feeling." She pulled back and stared into her friend's eyes. "I'm scared shitless right now."

"I've been picking up strange vibes today myself. Hell, it happens every crabbing season, but with the *Northern Star's* mayday this morning, I've been running every chant, prayer and spell I can think of to bring all of them back safe—your hubby included."

Jolene smiled. Madison was the very first person she met when after moving to Kodiak and the only other Wiccan in town. They became fast friends and soon the bond between them was second only to that she shared with her husband. She was grateful to have Madison to lean on, especially now with the baby only weeks away. "I don't know what I'd do without you."

"Well, you'll never have to find out. I'm here for the long haul, sugar. I'll be right there holding your hand until Steve pushes me out of the way—after our group hug of course. You know I love me some squeezing from that sexy man of yours. Ummmhumm!"

Jolene's bawdy laughter echoed off the wall. "Thanks. The thought of you in the middle of the two of us getting squeezed within an inch of your life and loving every single minute of it made my entire week. That's why I love you so much." She threw her arms around her friend and squeezed tightly. "I owe you a proper hug once the bambino decides to move out of his current residence."

Madison held her at arm's length and stared at her with a look of disbelief. "You said you wanted to wait until he was born before finding out the sex. You stinker!"

She laughed again. "Relax, woman. I didn't let the doctors tell me. I take turns calling out boy and girl names to see what fits. He gets most active with the masculine names, you know, with his happy kicks across my belly? Only little half-hearted punches occur with the feminine names."

"Sounds good to me, but I have to admit I was hoping for another Little Jo to take under my wing. We need three of us to make powerful magic in this town. Try as he might, Steve is just not sexy witch material."

Jolene's knees buckled as a wave of nausea slammed through her body.

"Jolene! Someone get a gurney! Honey, what's wrong?"

"Dizzy. I feel like I'm spinning out of control." She clutched her friend's arm and struggled to her feet. "Oh God. I'm going to be sick." She barely made it to the trash can in the hallway before losing all the food she'd forced herself to eat during day.

"Where the hell's that gurney? We need a doctor. Now!"

* * * *

Tammy Dennings Maggy

CHAPTER 4

December 22nd, Present Day Bering Sea,
East of St. Matthew Island, Alaska

The slow rhythmic thump of the helo blades grew louder as it approached Steve's location. Relief washed over him as the red and white helicopter came around to get into position to be able to lower the hoist line. The waves threatened to capsize the raft a few times since the first rescue team left him alone. The connection with the second team had cut in and out for the last ten minutes. He assumed the range of the transistor was being affected by the storm blowing through the area. No matter now. It was time to get the hell out of there. *Thank you, Lady. I knew you'd keep me safe.*

Suddenly, all the static from the radio cleared. "Jesus! Look at the size—"

Tammy Dennings Maggy

He looked out the opening of the raft to see the helicopter rise rapidly. Only one thing could make the pilot cut away like that.

Rogue waves.

He dropped the radio, grabbed the ropes and straps nearest to him, and braced for impact.

The radio came to life again. "Hold on, Steve. We're—"

He didn't hear anything else as the raft flipped over with such force, the air rushed out of his lungs after he crashed into the roof of the raft.

Before he could catch his breath and right himself, the raft was hit again and sailed through the air. He lost his hold on the first set of ropes as his body and the raft became airborne. He frantically searched for anything to hang onto, and braced himself for the inevitable free fall back down into the ocean and the murderous waves. As soon as he hit, another wave slammed into the raft, nearly crushing him under the weight of it. The radio crackled to life one more time before he blacked out and felt nothing.

* * * *

"Swimmer down! Rogue wave crashed over the raft. Lost visual and COMM. Repeat. Lost visual of raft. Swimmer down!"

Chief Petty Officer Bryant stared out at the churning Bering Sea, unable to believe his friend vanished in front of his eyes. "Come around again. Get in lower. I can't see shit!"

The pilot brought them in as low as he dared with the waves now cresting at well over seventy feet. Bryant had never witnessed three rogue waves crash over any vessel in such quick succession. Sure there were the stories from the fisherman, but to see it up close and personal turned his blood to ice. *He can't be gone. There's no way in hell I'm going to let the Bering Sea Bitch take him. Not now. Not ever.*

The helo circled one more time before widening the search grid. He kept his eyes on the waves, looking for any sign of the bright orange covered raft. If it flipped and ended upside down on the waves, he'd be hard pressed to spot it unless Steve could right it again. If injured, he'd be unable to pull on the straps inside and the raft would quickly take on water.

He tried one more time to get any response over the emergency channel from his friend. "Steve, if you can hear me we're coming for you. Hang on."

"Chief? We need a cutter out here and any available vessels to keep their eyes out for both rafts. Four fisherman are still missing along with our swimmer."

"Send the call out."

"COMSTA Kodiak. This is RESCUE Helicopter Charlie 9954. We've lost visual of rescue swimmer. Still no contact with second *Northern Star* life raft. Need assistance of any and all vessels in the area."

"Roger. Cutter *Sherman* fifteen nautical miles west of your position will join the search. Alert to all available fishing vessels in the area to go out momentarily. COMSTA Kodiak out."

Momentarily? What the hell are they waiting for? He kept his thoughts to himself, resisting the urge to verbally throttle the radio operator on the other end of their communications. The last thing any of them needed was for him to lose focus on the job at hand.

The weather and the sea weren't their only enemies on this trip. If they didn't find the remaining lost fisherman and Steve within the next forty-eight hours, their rescue mission would be classified as recovery. To him, that meant no hope of survival and he wasn't about to give up on his friend.

The *Sherman* had its own HH-65 Dolphin rescue helicopter on board. With them involved in the search, they'd be able to cover more ground in less time if the weather cooperated. With the winds and the waves, the conditions were getting too dangerous to continue the search by air. It all had to be done by the cutters and the other fishing vessels in the area.

Bryant scanned the churning waters once more before sliding back into his seat and restraints. He sighed and closed his eyes in silent prayer. *This is the sort of thing we all accept can happen when we signed up for this job, but please…please don't take him this way. He needs to come back home to his wife and newborn. He's saved so many. Can you at least give him that?*

* * * *

December 22nd, Present Day Kodiak Island

"I'm so scared, Mad. What if something is really wrong with the baby? It's happened before—"

"Stop that right now, Jolene Abigail Sanders. You and your son have come this far together, there's no way in hell the Goddess would take him from you now."

She sobbed. "I need Steve. I can't go through this again."

"Shh, now. We'll Skype with him as soon as he gets back to Cold Bay. You know they can't contact him when he's out on a rescue, sweetie."

Jolene shook her head. "He's in trouble out there. I can feel it. If he doesn't come back soon, I'm going to lose him forever to that damn sea. We made a deal, Mad. He promised to always come back to me, but something's wrong."

"Honey, you have to calm down before your blood pressure gets any higher. It's not good for you or the baby." Madison wrapped her arms around her and held her tight as they rocked together in the bed. "I know you're scared, but you have to think of the baby now. Keep your mind focused on him and breathe with me, okay?"

She took a deep breath and held it a few seconds before slowly letting it out. "I felt something change between us. I've always been able to feel Steve with me. Always. Not now. All I feel is cold and black." Her heart rate shot up again. She couldn't concentrate on keeping calm knowing her husband was hours away and possibly hurt—or worse.

"I'll see what I can find out, Jo. You just take care of yourself and the baby. Let me worry about Steve for you." The Coast Guard Chaplain stood at the end of her bed, his eyes filled with concern.

She hadn't realized he was in the room until he'd spoken. The soothing timbre of his voice calmed her a bit more. Together, they'd helped bring comfort to so many wives and families of missing fisherman over the years. Now it was her turn. "I'll do my best. Please. If there's any news at all, you have to tell me right away. Don't hold anything back."

The Chaplain closed his eyes and nodded. "When I know something, you'll know it. I promise."

One of the nurses entered the room with a catheter kit. "Doc wants me to hook you up with her special cocktail. With all you've been through today, you've made yourself a bit dehydrated. Can't have that now can we?"

Jolene smiled. "No we can't. You're all right. I need to concentrate on the baby and me. There's no point in getting myself this worked up when we have no idea what's going on out there. Right?"

Madison hugged her one more time before letting her go. "Right. Now how about I give you and Nurse Sunshine here some privacy to get your fluids set up? I'll be outside in the hallway. I need to talk to the Chaplain before he heads over to see the commander about your hubby."

* * * *

"You and I have known Jolene for over ten years. Have you ever once seen her have this emotional reaction to Steve being out on a rescue?" The Chaplain leaned against the wall down the hall from their friend's room. "If she doesn't calm down, I fear for her baby's survival."

Madison shook her head. "She's never been like this, not even when she miscarried the last baby. She had to go through that alone, but she never faltered. She's the strongest woman I know. That's why I'm scared. The two of them really do have a connection, you know."

"How so?"

"I believe in soul mates, padre. I've not met mine yet, but I know he or she's out there waiting for me. Those two are the real deal. They experience each other's emotions, illnesses, and sometimes can hear each other's thoughts. She told me once that it's not like either one can actually read minds, but the feelings behind their thoughts are shared."

The Chaplain nodded. "Like being an empath. I've seen a bit of that in my travels. I didn't realize the two of them shared that. They're truly blessed to have one another in this lifetime."

"Yes, they are. Right now, it's up to us to be sure she concentrates on that blessing until we find him. She's not one we can keep any information from for too long, but would you mind talking with me before you tell her what you find out? Together we can figure out how to tell her what's going on without sending her over the edge again."

"Good idea. Even if I tried, I'd never be able to keep anything from her. She'd see through it in a heartbeat. It's what makes her such a compassionate nurse and friend." He glanced at his watch and sighed. "I'd better get rolling if I want to catch the commander in his office. He's supposed to be on a plane this afternoon back to the mainland to attend some family thing for the holidays. It's my impression he's really not looking forward to going."

Madison laughed. "From what I hear, he prefers to stay here in Kodiak or anywhere his in-laws are *not*. Call me as soon as you find out anything."

* * * *

Tammy Dennings Maggy

CHAPTER 5

December 23rd, Middle of the Bering Sea, location unknown

Steve awakened to find the raft upright and miraculously not filled with water. How the hell he made it out of the crushing force of the waves that had crashed into him moments before he blacked out, he'll never know. *Maybe I didn't make it and this is some sort of cruel cosmic joke?*

Untangling himself from the straps he'd wrapped his fingers around before the raft tumbled out of control turned into a major project in and of itself. His muscles had locked in position from the adrenaline that still coursed through his body. The last thing he remembered was hearing a voice through the radio speaker yelling about the size of something. Moments later, he had the air squeezed out of his lungs from the powerful force of not one, but two waves colliding against the raft, nearly crushing him to death in the process.

He had no idea how long he was out, or if he was anywhere near his last coordinates. It didn't matter. He knew after forty-eight hours they'd be looking to recover his body. With any luck at all, some fishing vessel would spot the raft and help him. Unfortunately, he realized the odds of that happening grew slimmer with each passing hour. It's damn hard to see a raft in bad weather during daylight, but now only pitch black surrounded him.

Slowly flexing and extending his fingers, he stimulated blood circulation in them. Continuing to work his way up his arms, legs and finally neck he didn't find any obvious injuries besides the painful throb in his lower back. Since he had feeling in his legs and could move them, he didn't think it was broken, but couldn't rule out a partially slipped disk. Of course until found and safely back to base, there was no way in hell he'd take off the survival wet suit to look at the bruising he was sure covered him from head to toe.

The constant roaring of the high winds and waves crashing around the raft turned into the Bering Sea version of white noise. Most people would go batty listening to the storm rage around them in the dark, but not Steve. For him, the smells and sounds of the ocean when at its worst filled him with a calm and wonder. Even though he knew the danger, he didn't fear it. Death at sea wouldn't be unexpected, and in fact, he hoped it would be the way he'd go when it was time.

His thoughts turned to Jolene and the baby they'd worked so hard to bring to this world. They'd talked about this sort of thing on many occasions. Each time it always ended up with him promising he'd return to her. Both knew the promise may one day have to be broken, and that part devastated him.

"I'm sorry, babe. This may be time I have to break my vow. I hope you'll forgive me one day."

A wave of nausea hit him like a ton of brinks. Barely making it to the raft's small opening, he braced himself only seconds before his stomach clenched and forced out the remainder of his last meal into the churning water. The only other time he'd had that kind of reaction was when Jolene was bedridden with morning sickness. A cold fear gripped his heart like a vice. *Could she feel what I'd gone through with the waves? No, no, no! She had to stay calm and keep the baby safe.*

He leaned back to rest his head against the side of the raft, and curled up into the fetal position, praying with all his might his wife could hear him somehow and know he was alive and doing everything he could to get back to her. Never mind the odds weren't in his favor. He needed to believe with his heart and soul he'd make it back to her arms. "Jo. I'm here honey. I'm right there with you. I'll always be with you no matter what. Never forget that. Hold on to our love and help me come home to you."

His heart rate sped up and his temples pounded with the telltale signs his blood pressure was on the rise. Although he had enough reasons for his blood pressure to skyrocket, only one concerned him the most. "You have to calm down, honey. It's not good for the baby or you. Please, hear me."

* * * *

December 23rd, Present Day, Kodiak Island

She drifted in and out of sleep. In her dreams she'd watched Steve drown over and over again. Each time she reached for him, his fingers were just out of reach and he sank beneath the waves, lost to her forever.

The alarms on the monitors shrilled loudly bringing her up out of the last horrible dream. Two nurses rushed into the room, followed by her obstetrician, Dr. Jillian Norris. "Jolene, I'm going to have to give you a light sedative to calm you down. You're blood pressure's much too high and you're putting your little one at risk. You've come all this way together. Let's not make the last part of his journey into this world harder than it has to be."

"No. Please. I just want my husband. Can someone tell me what the hell's going on with him? It's been over twelve hours. Why haven't we heard anything yet?" Tears streamed down her face. "I can't feel him anymore. Something's wrong."

Dr. Norris injected the medication into her intravenous line, completely ignoring her objections. "Your friends are already working on getting information for you. I understand how upset you are—"

Jolene glared and hissed through her teeth. "Do you? Is your partner out in the middle of a storm on a rescue mission? Do you live with the fear your partner will never come back to you each time they go out into those hell waters? Well? Do you? I'm sick and tired of people telling me to calm down. I'm going out of my ever loving mind with worry here."

You have to calm down, honey. It's not good for the baby or you. Please, hear me.

Steve? Her mind reached out to her husband, trying to connect with him again but was met with only silence. She closed her eyes tightly and took several deep, cleansing breaths before opening them again.

Everyone stared at her with shock on their faces. Mortified by her own outburst, she covered her mouth and shook her head. More tears fell down her cheeks. "I'm so sorry. I didn't mean...I'm not..."

Dr. Norris took her hand and squeezed tightly. "You're going to get through this. Both you and the baby. You have to trust me to take care of the both of you until Steve comes back. I made a promise to him to watch over *you* while he was away and I'll be damned if I'll let your stubbornness prevent me from doing that."

She wiped the tears from her face and laughed. "Well, I guess that's that. I promise to stop being the patient from hell long enough for you to do what you need to do to take care of the baby." She settled back against her pillows as the sedative started to make everything fuzzy around the edges. For the first time that night, the tension in her body eased up a bit.

Once again she reached out to Steve, hoping against all hope he could hear her. *I'm trying to calm down, honey, but you don't make it easy on a gal. Now hurry home. There's a cluster of mistletoe in our living room that has our names on it.*

* * * *

CHAPTER 6

December 25th, Eighteen years ago
Remote cabin in Northern Michigan

Steve unlocked the front door before turning back to his bride of only twelve hours. He scooped her up into his arms and kissed her again. "Welcome to our home away from home, Mrs. Sanders."

Her eyes widened as he sat her on her booted feet. "When did you have time to get this all set up?"

He watched her as she walked around the room. The caretakers had come in the hour before to be sure everything was perfect. They started the now roaring welcome fire in the fireplace and set a bottle of chilled champagne and two classes out on the coffee table along with a platter of meats, cheese and fruit. "This is just the beginning. Come with me."

He took her hand in his and kissed it gently before he led her into the next room. "Here we have the kitchen with a fully stocked pantry for your cooking pleasure."

"Or yours." Jolene squeezed his fingers and smiled.

"Of course. I have a couple new dishes I'd like to surprise you with this trip." He kissed her again and pulled her to the next room. "Come on, if I don't get you out of here, you'll start rifling through all the cupboards and planning menus."

He twirled her around the hallway to get her to laugh. The sound tickled his ears and caused his stomach to do little flutters every time he heard it. It's what got him through basic training and what will get him through his first tour away from her in a few short weeks. Until then, they had fourteen glorious days alone at the cabin to just get lost in each other.

"Oh! It's beautiful!" They'd made it to the door of the master bedroom to find winter rose petals strewn all over the bed and the floor. Another fire blazed in the room's small fireplace. At least a dozen fat white candles emitted soft glowing light, filling the room with vanilla and lavender scents.

"Do you like it? I wasn't sure what to do in here, but your bridesmaids helped me get it right. The folks who rent this place out told me they'd never had so much fun getting the cabin ready for new guests. I guess it's the first time someone spent their honeymoon here."

Her eyes filled with tears. "This is the sweetest thing anyone's ever done for me...for us. It's almost too beautiful to sleep in."

"Oh, there will be very little sleeping done in that bed tonight!" He raised his eyebrows up and down rapidly before he spun her around again and into the dramatic dip he'd practiced for weeks for their first dance as man and wife.

Once again, her giggles grabbed his heart and brought another smile to his face. "I have one more surprise for you before we dive into that champagne and food out in the living room."

"Another surprise? This is all more than enough for me, babe." She wrapped her arms around his waist and tightly hugged him, her head rested just under his chin. "Being able to have you all to myself for a bit before I have to share you with our families and the Coast Guard is the best Christmas gift I could ever hope for."

"Getting married at the stroke of midnight ensured I'd never forget our wedding anniversary. You're a genius."

Jolene tilted her head to look into his eyes. A Cheshire cat grin formed on her lips. "Yes, I am. Besides, I wanted to incorporate our mistletoe promise in our vows."

"Speaking of that, follow me." He slipped out of her arms and bolted out of the bedroom and down the hallway to a door he'd yet to open for her. He turned to see her only steps behind him. "Close your eyes."

She immediately did as he asked and linked her arm with his. "Lead the way, Mr. Sanders."

He opened the door and brought her into the room before closing the door behind them. "Okay, open them."

She gasped. Before them a large four-person hot tub bubbled to life in the middle of a glass walled room. The hardwood floors were covered with various thick shag rugs. One wall had shelves filled with large fluffy towels and two thick robes hung on hooks next to the door. Outside the snow fell and created huge drifts in the wind, while inside was toasty warm. "I can't believe you found a place like this. It's amazing!"

"Look up." He pointed a remote control at the glass ceiling. As they watched, a large bouquet of mistletoe wrapped in red velvet ribbons lowered to rest over the hot tub. "There are special heating coils in the ceiling to keep the glass clear of snow. You said you've always fantasized about making love under the stars. Well, in this room we can do it, in or out of the hot tub." He winked and smiled. "What do you think? Did I do good?"

She nodded and threw her arms around his neck.

He lifted her off her feet and crushed her against his chest as his mouth found her warm and wanting lips. His tongue glided over hers, as she lifted her legs to wrap around his hips. His hands slid down to her tight ass and dug his fingers into the painted on jeans covering it. "I want to feel your skin next to mine. As sexy as you look in these clothes, I can't wait any longer to get you out of them."

* * * *

"What's stopping you?" Jolene combed her fingers through her husband's hair and pulled his head back. She ran her tongue from his Adam's apple, up over his stubbly chin, and back to his demanding lips. She couldn't get enough of his kisses.

With only his lips and tongue he had the ability turn her into a puddle of molten goo. First he teased her with the slip and slide of his tongue over hers, drawing her in deeper and deeper before he took possession. He sucked her tongue hard before pulling back to catch her lower lip in his teeth.

Steve sat her down on the bench next to the hot tub and knelt down to remove first one boot and then the other before shedding himself of his down vest and hiking boots.

She smiled and stood to remove her own heavy winter coat and tossed it aside. She tugged at his belt buckle as he lifted his sweatshirt over his head and sent it to lay next to her jacket. Her hands tenderly roamed over his abs and then his chest as his muscles rippled and flexed beneath her fingertips. "I've been waiting all day to touch you like this."

"You and me both. His fingers worked her shirt free of her jeans and yanked it over her head in one motion before he pulled her back into his arms again.

Her nipples, already rock hard, strained against the red lace holding her tits in place. She rubbed her chest against his as her hands slipped through his open fly to caress his bulging cock. "Commando? Oh, aren't we naughty?"

He chuckled as his lips trailed down her neck, creating a buzzing sensation on her skin that left her weak in the knees. The deep rumble in his chest further tickled her nipples leaving them hypersensitive and her pussy clenching with need. Seeming to sense her torture, he expertly opened the clasps of her bra.

"You know what seeing you in red lace does to me." He hooked his thumbs in the straps and edged them over her shoulders and down her arms until the lingerie fell away. His hands cupped her firm round breasts and squeezed them together in order to take both nipples into his mouth at once. His tongue swirled around them quickly before biting down enough to make her gasp.

Her head fell back as she clung to his biceps and dug her nails into his flesh. "Don't stop, baby."

He popped one nipple out of his mouth, while continuing to suck harder on the other. Squeezing and kneading the breast he suckled while he slid his other hand down over her left hip and pealed her jeans away from her bare skin, leaving her now only in the red lace thong that matched her bra.

She pushed him away long enough to shove his jeans over his hips, freeing his dick. She sunk to her knees, grasped his shaft in one of her hands and popped the mushroomed head into her mouth.

He moaned and thrust his hips toward her, but Jolene held him in place with a tighter grip on his length, while her other hand fondled his balls. Round and round she swirled her tongue around the tip of his cock while her right hand moved up and down in the rhythm she knew made him weak in the knees. As salty pre-cum coated her tongue, she plunged down to take nearly all of satiny flesh into her mouth and throat.

He entangled his fingers in her hair and pushed it back from her face. She knew he loved to watch her suck him off. She opened her eyes wide and gazed up at him as she moved her mouth, hands and tongue up and down, and around his cock.

He thrust against her again and this time she allowed him to fuck her mouth through her hand, alternating the pressure around it with each of his thrusts and when he pulled back. She let him direct the speed for a few minutes more before she popped his dick out of her mouth and smiled up at him.

She scooted away from him on the plush rug, never breaking eye contact as she laid back. She lifted her hips to be able to wiggle herself out of her thong.

"Oh, no you don't. That's my job." He knelt between her legs and slid his hands slowly up her calves and thighs. Finally, he reached the thin thong straps on her hips. He grasped each side and snapped the panties from her now dripping cunt.

* * * *

Steve shoved her thighs apart and immediately dove in to claim his prize. As soon as he parted her swollen outer pussy lips, her clit snapped out of its little hood and appeared to pulse before his eyes. He flicked it once, twice and then a third time before sealing his lips over it.

Her hips bucked up off the floor. "Yes, yes, yes..."

Her mewling cries turned to moans as he sucked harder on her clit and thrust two fingers into her tight hole, curling them over her upper walls to find her trigger.

As soon as he pressed it, she arched her back and his hand was immediately covered with more of her sweet cum. He stiffened his tongue and dipped it into her folds over and over again, lapping up all the juices she continued to squirt out of her.

She cried out again as his lips found her clit once more. He swirled his tongue around the sensitive tissue rapidly as he lifted her legs so they rested on his shoulders. Now he wrapped his arms around both of her hips, holding her in place as he feasted on her entire pussy.

She tossed her head side to side and clenched her thighs tight around his head as yet another orgasm flew through her body. "I can't…Jesus Christ, I can't take much more."

He moved up her body, taking his time to kiss, lick and suck every sweet and salty bit in his path toward her mouth. He braced himself on one elbow as he held her face in his other hand. His thumb traced over her swollen lower lip before he kissed her, gently at first but then with more urgency.

Jolene wrapped her arms around his neck as he rolled them so she was now on top of him, her nipples crushed against his chest. She opened her eyes and held his gaze as she sat up. Her nails trailed down his chest as she slid down his body, grinding her wet cunt into him every inch of the way.

He thrust his cock up toward her, slipping between her legs and her slick mound, but not into her as he wanted.

She laughed and shook her head. "Can't a girl catch her breath a moment and enjoy the feel of her husband beneath her?" She wiggled lower and raised herself above his hips, just out of reach.

"Damn it, woman. I thought you couldn't take much more of me eating you out and here you are teasing the hell out of me." He smiled, suddenly sat up and pulled her back into his arms again.

She eased herself down over his cock and sighed as she took all of him deep inside her. She rocked her hips first front to back and then side to side, before wrapping her legs around his waist.

His hands slid down her lower back and over her firm bubble shaped ass. His fingers dug into her flesh as he lifted her up and down his dick. He enjoyed the feel of her inner muscles clenching around him, pulling his cock deeper and deeper with each movement

She moaned as he picked up speed. "Harder, baby...harder."

He lifted her almost completely off before impaling her over and over again. Although he loved having her in his arms this way, something wasn't quite right and his own orgasm refused to follow any of hers.

She grasped his face in her hands and kissed him hard, completely melting in his arms as yet another wave of ecstasy zipped through her body.

He leaned back toward the floor and flipped her onto her back. He knelt up and pulled out of her before quickly turning her over onto her stomach.

She propped up on her hands and knees. She giggled when he grabbed her hips and pulled her toward him.

He pushed her shoulders toward the floor, forcing her ass high up in the air. Her pussy glistened and begged him to fuck her. He knelt and ran his tongue through her wet folds and up toward her ass and back again. He shoved his tongue into her cunt as his thumb rolled over her clit repeatedly.

She squealed and thrust her hips back toward him, shoving his tongue deeper into her. Her thighs quivered as more cum flowed from her pussy, signaling she was primed and ready for more.

He stroked his throbbing cock a few times as he positioned the head at her entrance. He thrust into her fully and held her there a moment before covered her body with his own. He braced himself his hands on the bench in front of them and pumped into her with wild abandon.

He looked up at their reflection in the glass wall in front of them. Jolene's eyes were closed and her face cheeks a deep crimson, as she rocked back toward him meeting every plunge of his dick. She had never looked more beautiful to him. His heart overflowed with love for her and the need to take all she was willing to give. He plunged into her even harder as his balls contracted and he finally went over the edge with his wife.

* * * *

CHAPTER 7

December 23rd, Present Day, Middle of the Bering Sea

"Mayday, mayday, mayday. This is Petty Officer Sanders on life raft from the *Northern Star.* Last known location was east of St. Matthew Island before hit by rogue waves. Anyone out there?"

No response but static. He'd tried the same message at least once every fifteen minutes after awakening. At least he was getting static now. That was new since the day before.

As far as he could tell, it had been about six hours since dawn. With the storm clouds still overhead and blocking out the sun, he had a hell of a time trying to get his bearings. At first light he was able to find his flashlight that had come out of his survival suit while he was being tossed around the waves like a rag doll. A thorough search of all the pockets revealed another surprise—two energy bars and one-liter bag of intravenous Lactated Ringers solution. While not ideal, he could drink it in a pinch as long as he did it slowly.

After securing his supplies in his pockets, he sent out the mayday once again before sitting back to conserve some of his energy and concentrate on Jolene. His dreams throughout the night focused on their wedding night and honeymoon.

It was during their time in that secluded northern Michigan cabin when they'd had unprotected sex for the first time. Prior to that, they'd always been careful. Jolene had graduated from high school only six months before and was enrolled in nursing program at Saginaw Valley State University at the time of their wedding.

He himself had only been out of high school two years. He'd joined the Coast Guard the day after graduation. Eight weeks later, he found himself assigned to the US Coast Guard Cutter Mackinaw. It was with that crew he found his love of Search and Rescue and had applied to—and been accepted into—the swimmer training school.

Being away from her for over five months damn near killed him and filled him with guilt leaving the wedding planning up to her. Lucky for him, she didn't seem to mind that part. That's why he took such pains to make sure their honeymoon was extra special and a huge surprise for her.

As it turned out, both were in for another surprise a month later when she'd found out she was pregnant. Although the timing wasn't the greatest, they were over the moon with the idea of having a baby. Unfortunately, two months later she miscarried while Steve was had been on a mission rescuing fisherman trapped on an ice flow that had broken free of the shoreline of the Upper Peninsula.

* * * *

April 15th, Eighteen Years Ago
Small Town in Central Michigan

Steve carefully drove through the slush filled back roads near the Saginaw Valley State University campus. The weather in Michigan never ceased to amaze him. One day it's all sunshine and flowers starting to bloom, and the next it's three inches of snow overnight. The end result covered the I-75 and had slowed his progress for most of his trip home. Now he was within five minutes of scooping his wife up in his arms and holding her tight. He could barely contain his excitement to concentrate on the slippery road.

Soon all the ice, snow and slush would melt away as the spring rains rolled in. This was his favorite time of year. To him, spring meant new beginnings. He couldn't think of a better way to celebrate that then to be able to tell friends and family about the baby.

If he had his way, he would've shouted from the rooftops the moment the little home pregnancy test turned blue, but she had wanted to keep it their secret for a bit. She didn't want her family in particular to chastise them for getting pregnant so soon after getting married. Her mother had even gone so far as to give them a huge box of condoms for a wedding present. Jolene had been mortified, but he had only laughed it off and said his new mother in law was just too young to be a grandmother.

He'd kept his promise and their secret until now. This was the time they'd agreed upon to tell everyone they were going to be parents. It was hard to keep the secret when his own parents called him for their weekly chats while he lived on base in Cheboygan over the last three months away from home.

They agreed it was better for her to live closer to school so she could finish up her nursing degree. Once that was completed, she'd be a Registered Nurse and could find a job wherever the Coast Guard chose to send him. Still, being separated for three months and home for one was hard on anyone, but especially newlyweds expecting their first child.

No sooner had he pulled up in front of their little townhouse, the front door flew open. Jolene rushed into his arms and held on for dear life. He body trembled against his.

"I missed you too, babe." He whispered in her ear and kissed her cheek. That's when he tasted the salty tears on her skin. "What's wrong, Jo?"

The sobs tore through her body and she held on tighter.

He carried her back into the house, leaving his gear in the car. That could wait. His wife was more important. He sat her down on the couch and took her hands in his as he knelt next to her on the floor. "Babe, please tell me what's made you so upset. Is it your mom again?"

She shook her head. "I wish it was. I went to the doctor today because I started spotting. She couldn't find a heartbeat. I lost the baby. I'm...I'm so sorry."

His stomach twisted into a knot. "I don't understand. How—?"

She shook her head slowly. "She said there's nothing wrong with me physically. She spouted off a bunch of figures of how common it is for woman to miscarry during the first and even early second trimester. I already know that shit. I don't care about those other women. I wanted to know why I couldn't carry our baby."

He pulled her onto his lap and held her as another round of sobs racked her body. He gently rocked her and rubbed her back. Unable to hold back his own tears, he let them fall. Together they grieved for the loss of their child.

"Do you know what her nurse said to me as I was leaving?"

"What?" He reached for the box of tissues on the coffee table in front of them and offered them to her first.

She grabbed several and wiped his cheeks first before grabbing more to blow her nose. "She said, well you and your husband are young. You can always have more children, Jolene. There's no point in obsessing over why you lost this one. Hundreds of women every single day miscarry without knowing why. They accept it just wasn't meant to be. Can you believe that shit? She must've missed the sensitivity training classes when she went through nursing school. I just wanted to punch her in the face!"

He chuckled and then outright laughed. "Now that's something I'd pay to see."

She smiled. "I love your laugh."

"And I love you." He kissed her gently before she settled her head back down on his shoulder. "I wish you didn't have to go through all of this alone, honey."

"You're doing what you're supposed to be doing, saving lives. There was nothing you could have done to stop this from happening. I felt you with me today even though you weren't here in the flesh."

"I think I may have sensed something was wrong with you. I didn't know it at the time, but while coming back to base after the mission, I had an overwhelming need to see you and hear your voice."

"I'm glad you got here when you did. I felt so alone in that office. Then to have that nurse more or less tell me to buck up and try again, I fell apart."

He tilted her chin so she had to look up at him. His heart broke again at the sight of her eyes filled with sorrow and guilt. "It's okay to fall apart, honey but you have to stop blaming yourself. You didn't do anything wrong. I don't know why this happened, but we'll get through it together. We lost a little piece of us and it hurts like hell."

She reached up and tenderly placed her hand over his cheek. "I knew you'd understand. Hey, you told me you had a surprise for me when you got home. What was it?"

"Well, I found this cute little t-shirt in the exchange and I just had to buy it." He bit his lower lip to keep it from quivering. "It was for the baby."

She got up off his lap and pulled him up from the couch. "Show me."

* * * *

December 23rd, Present Day, Middle of the Bering Sea

Steve remembered the look on her face when he showed her the little mint green shirt. She squealed and smiled for the first time since he'd arrived home. On the front was a little cartoon bear in swim gear with the words "Future Coast Guard Swimmer." On the back it read "Just like my daddy." Instead of making her sad, the piece of baby clothing gave her hope that one day they would be parents.

Eighteen years later they were one month away from realizing that dream and here he was stranded in the middle of the Bering Sea. Jolene had once again gone through the ups and downs of her pregnancy without him.

If he wasn't found soon, she'd have to go through the rest of her life without him, too. That's what all Coasties sign up for when they join, but not Jolene. It wasn't fair she had to worry about him and the baby now, too

The Great Lakes are some of the most dangerous waters in the country and he learned a hell of a lot during his eight years there while Jolene finished her degree and worried about him constantly. She packed up everything and gladly left behind all her friends and family to move to Kodiak to be nearby so he could continue to live his dream.

Both of their lives changed dramatically the moment he reported for duty. Even the frigid tumultuous waters of Lake Superior couldn't prepare him for the hazards of being part of the

Search and Rescue teams stationed in Alaska. The Bering Sea showed no mercy and took no prisoners. Keeping the fishing fleets out of harm's way kept the Coasties busy and away from their families twenty four hours a day when they were on rotation.

There in the middle of hell, his dream had turned into a nightmare. Steve had finally met his match.

"I'm so sorry, Jo. If I make it out of this, I'll sit for the Chief's exam and let the younger petty officers take over the rotations." *I've put her through enough. It's time to think of retiring with that anchor on my collar.*

* * * *

Tammy Dennings Maggy

CHAPTER 8

December 24th, Present Day Kodiak, Alaska

Jolene twisted her wedding ring around and around on her finger. Steve had wanted to give her the band to match her engagement ring, but she'd had her heart set on a simple piece to match the one he'd wear. Together they searched until they found the perfect ones. They were made of simple white gold to match her diamond setting, but with the words *"Mo Anam Cara"* engraved on the outside.

Her mother teased her endlessly about the rings, calling them childish friendship bands worth less than two hundred bucks combined. Jolene tried to explain to her it wasn't how much they cost, but what they symbolized. Steve was her soul mate and best friend and she wanted to honor that in the rings they gave to each other.

"If you keep twisting your rings around you're going to spin them right off your finger. You know how bad my eyesight is. If they fly off, I may not be able to help you find them." Madison stretched out on the cot next to her raised hospital bed and smiled. "How long have you been awake?"

"Only about an hour now. It's a few minutes after midnight. The night crew came in a few moments ago to check my stats. My blood pressure's still a little high but Doc's no longer threatening to take me to Anchorage with her this morning."

"Well, you were giving all of us quite the scare there for a while. This small town hospital's okay for the general stuff, but they aren't prepared to do a C-section. You're damn lucky Jillian flew in yesterday to watch over you, otherwise you and I would be having this conversation in the big hospital."

She nodded and sighed. "I heard Steve's voice in my dreams telling me to keep calm and take care of myself and the baby. He's alive out there. I can feel him."

Madison rubbed her eyes. "I believe you, honey. If anyone can survive out there for this long, it's your husband but—"

"But what? It's been over thirty-six hours since the *Northern Star* sent out the mayday. Another twelve hours and the Coast Guard won't be searching for survivors anymore. He has to hang on a little while longer."

"The Chaplain said they brought in four of fisherman late this afternoon into St. Paul. They should be arriving here in Kodiak in the morning. Maybe we can get a bit more information from them about what happened out there."

She closed her eyes and took a deep breath. "Four survivors?"

Her friend nodded. "Yeah. I assumed there were four in each raft. One's still missing."

"I have a pretty good idea what happened. If Steve's team brought in four at once, there wouldn't be any room on board for him. Protocol dictates the swimmer be left behind if more than three survivors are brought on board the helicopter. They'd either come back for him or a second crew would pick him up. I always wondered what would happen if he were left behind and something went wrong. Now I know."

Madison got up from the cot and sat next to her. She reached for both of her hands and tightly grasped them. "No you don't know what happened. Twelve hours is a hell of a long time yet. The entire crab fleet's joined the search for Steve and the second raft. They'll be found, I'm sure of it."

Jolene squeezed Madison's hands. "I don't know what I'd do without you. I'm having such a hard time dealing with this. I've never been more scared for him out there alone. What if he doesn't come back, Mad? What the hell am I going to do without him?" Her eyes stung with fresh tears.

"I'm not going to let you go down that path, Jo. Until we know for sure, you can't give up on him. He'll keep fighting to get back to you as long as he can feel your connection. Hold on to that with all you have. I'll lend my energy to your prayers to the Goddess to bring him back. You know all your friends are already praying for his safe return. Tap into that energy to give you the strength to see this through."

"It's hard to do that when every time I close my eyes, I see him being slammed by waves and taken under. Drowning's my own worst fear. Not for him. Sometimes I wonder how we got together with my fear of the water and the sea being his first love."

"There you go. It's your own fears coming to you in your dreams, not what's really happening to him. The Lady of the Sea may be his first love, but you are his heart and soul. You and your son growing inside you, waiting for the right time to make his appearance, are Steve's reason for living. I believe with all my heart The Lady won't take either of them from you now—not when you're so close to having the family you've always longed to have."

I'm coming home, Jo. I'll meet you under the mistletoe just like always.

She tilted her head and stared at her friend. "Did you hear that?"

"No. I only hear the sound of your monitors." Madison arched one eyebrow and looked around the room.

I'm coming home, Jo. Meet me under the mistletoe..."

Jolene smiled through her tears. "It's Steve. He's coming home."

* * * *

December 24th, Middle of the Bering Sea

"Mayday, mayday, mayday. This is Petty Officer Steve Sanders on a raft from the *Northern Star*. Anyone out there?"

He called out the mayday at least once every thirty minutes now, or as close as he could. Without his watch or any other electronics besides the portable transistor radio, he had no way of knowing the actual time. His best guess was it was a little after midnight on Christmas Eve, but that all depended on how long he was knocked out by the waves after the rescue.

The radio crackled to life as he was about to send another call out. "This is the fishing vessel *Gypsea Queen*. We have you in sight and have notified Kodiak of our position."

A wave of relief flooded through his body. *Thank you, Goddess.* He pulled back the panel covering the opening of the raft and nearly wept with joy. "*Gypsea Queen,* you're a sight for sore eyes."

A deep chuckle came through the speaker. "The entire fleet's put fishing on hold to find you. You'll be happy to hear the remaining *Northern Star* crewmembers are on board and waiting to welcome you home."

"Roger that. Can't wait to head home with them. We've all got a lot of celebrating to do."

"Stand by as we come around and get close enough to lower the hook and bring you on board."

"Standing by." He watched the vessel slowly turn and begin its way back toward him. The lights flooded the deck and he could make out several fisherman along the rail armed with life rings. He glanced upward as the hook lowered toward the raft. *I'm coming home, Jo. I'll meet you under the mistletoe just like always.*

The hook finally made it low enough for him to step onto it. He wrapped his arms around the cold galvanized steel and gave the crew the thumbs up sign.

"Raise him up!" The three words rang out over the noise of the wind and the waves. His heart rate quickened. *It's really happening.*

All eyes were on him as the hook lifted him from the raft and the surface of the water. A cheer erupted as soon as his head and shoulders cleared the rail. Several hands pulled him onto the deck. Someone wrapped him in a thermal blanket and led him toward the wheelhouse. Warm dry clothes and more blankets were set out for him.

He tried to peel off his wet suit but found his muscles no longer obeyed his brain. "I could use a little help—"

"I gotcha, Steve. It's the least I can do for the man who got four of my crew home safe tonight." The captain of the *Northern Star* gripped his hand and shook it. "We wouldn't be here if it wasn't for your team and the rest of the crabbers."

"Fitz, I wouldn't have been able to contact anyone if you hadn't insisted your crew take the radios with them. Thank you. I thought it was my last mission."

The captain smiled. "Not on our watch. We'll get you home in time to bring in Christmas morning with your wife. Coast Guard cutter *Sherman* and their helo will be here within the hour and fly us back to St. Paul. Then it's on to—"

"Kodiak." The breath rushed out of his lungs as he said the name of his homeport. His vision blurred a bit as the room seemed to spin around him.

Fitz held onto Steve as his knees buckled. "Whoa. Let's get you out of this suit and see what the medic on board can do to get some fluids going in you. You've been out there for over thirty-six hours."

He nodded and let the older man undress him and wrap him in more thermal blankets. *I'm coming home, Jo. Meet me under the mistletoe at midnight.*

* * * *

.

CHAPTER 9

December 24th, Present Day Kodiak, Alaska

Jolene sat in her wheelchair and glanced around the little hospital chapel filled with her friends and coworkers. The four fisherman rescued nearly a day and a half ago sat in the back with their families. The chaplain stood in front of the first row of pews, greeting folks as they took their seats.

He smiled when he noticed her in the doorway and walked toward her. "I see Madison broke you out of your room to join us. We've been here praying for the safe return of your husband and the rest of the missing crew. The last update said they found both rafts and survivors but no other details yet."

"That's protocol. They have to be checked out in St. Paul first before they release any survivor details." She knew the drill. She'd explained it time and time again to the wives of the fisherman missing over the years. Now the words sounded hollow to her ears. Every single minute that passed without any word from Steve—or anyone for that matter intensified the anxiety flooding through her.

Madison patted her on the shoulder. "You don't have to be strong for everyone else now, sugar. We're all here for you. Look around the room again. What do you see?"

She did as her friend asked and gasped. "Where on earth did you find so much mistletoe?"

"The padre here called in a few favors and I have my own sources." Madison wheeled her toward the front of the chapel and helped her up from the chair so she could stand in front of the altar filled with candles.

"These are the exact same kind Steve and I had at our wedding. How did you know?"

"I told her."

She turned around at the sound of the familiar deep baritone. Her hands shook at her sides. She wasn't hallucinating. He was there in the doorway of the chapel. "When did you do that?"

Steve walked slowly down the aisle toward her. "Last week. I wanted to surprise you with a vow renewal. It's our eighteenth wedding anniversary, but it's been twenty-five years since you first agreed to kiss me under the mistletoe."

"You remembered." She smiled broadly and reached for him.

He crossed the last few feet and scooped her into his arms, holding her tight against his chest. "I'd never forget the day the only girl I'll ever love said yes." He placed her back on her feet and gazed

74

into her eyes. "So what do you say? Will you marry me again?"

"Yeah, Jo. What do you say?" Jake stood up and pointed to his watch. We've got fifteen minutes before midnight. I'm sure the chaplain won't mind if Maddie performed the ceremony."

"Not in the least. Come on, Jo. What do you say?" The chaplain sat down in the front pew and crossed his arms over his chest and grinned from ear to ear.

They were all in on this. Every last one of them. "How can I say no when you brought your own cheerleaders? Of course I'll marry you again. You're my Knight in Shining Armor, my heart and soul. I can't eat or sleep when you're gone."

"You're my heart, my soul, and my everything. I promised you the moon and stars and you gave me the world." Steve put his hand on her stomach as the baby kicked up a storm. "I feel ya, little one. Poppy's home for good now."

She placed both of her hands over his. "Is that what you want?"

He nodded. "It's time I let the younger swimmers get a taste of the action. I can't keep hogging all the glory now, can I?"

"We're all glad you did this time!" Fitz and his family filed into the chapel and took their seats next to the rest of the *Northern Star* families. "Seriously, the young blood will learn a lot with you teaching them all you know."

Jolene looked to her best friend and nodded. "Let's do this, Mad."

Madison smiled and held up a rope of braided white and red ribbon. "Hold your hands, right to right and left to left."

Steve's callused hands held hers as if afraid to let go. She didn't mind at all. He was finally home with her again to stay. Chills ran up and down her spine as Madison loosely tied the braid around their crossed wrists in a figure eight pattern. This was exactly how it was done during their handfasting all those years ago.

Madison placed her right hand on top of their wrists and her left below. "Steve wanted you to recite the same vows you did when you first married. I'm sure both of you will have no trouble remembering them word for word even now."

He nodded and smiled. "I wish to join my life with yours."

She cleared her throat and began the second verse. "To stand by your side and sleep in your arms."

"To be joy to your heart and food to your soul."

"To work as partners and live as a family."

"While we grow old together."

"I vow to love, honor and respect you."

"To hold you to my heart."

"But not bind you to my will."

"I promise to listen carefully and to speak the truth."

"To stay with you through struggles and pleasures."

"All the days of my life."

"Will you accept me and all that I am?" She held his gaze and her breath waiting for his answer.

"I will. Will you accept me and all that I am?" Tears fell down his flushed cheeks.

Her heart overflowed with love for the man before her. "I will."

Madison gently slipped the knotted ribbons from their wrists and placed it back into the carved wooden box Jolene had stored them in after their first wedding. "By the powers invested in me by the state of Alaska and the blessing of the Goddess Brigid and the Lady of the Sea, I now pronounce you spouses forever and ever. Blessed be. Go on. It's midnight. Kiss your bride."

He tilted her chin up to kiss her. They did it. Their promise to each other remained unbroken, there under the mistletoe.

The End

Tammy Dennings Maggy

ABOUT THE AUTHOR

Tammy Dennings Maggy is a best-selling, multi-published poet and erotic romance author with Siren Bookstrand and Sassy Vixen Publishing. Her writing explores many facets of romance from ultimate betrayal to finding your soul mate. Her poetry serves as a companion to her novels and has inspired entire series all on their own. Tammy and her alter egos Lia Michaels, Stephanie Ryan and Tawny Savage make up the core authors at Sassy Vixen Publishing and together they've created the shared-world series, Temptations Resort. Look for the first books in that series to come out in late 2016.

Now happily married to her own Muse and soul mate, she continues to live her dream and act as secretary to all her characters demanding to have their stories told.

Connect with Tammy

www.authortammydenningsmaggy.com
www.sassyvixenpublishing.net

Other Tales by Tammy Dennings Maggy

Now and Forever Series
For the Love of Quinn (Now and Forever 1)
The Island (Now and Forever 2)
The Surrender of Julia (Now and Forever 3)
Bound in Paradise (Now and Forever 3.5)
Coming 2016: My Love, My Friend (Now and Forever 4)

Kayne Legacy Series
The Courtship of the Vampyre (poetry)
Curse of the First Born Cain (Kayne Legacy 1)
Coming 2016: Legacy of the First Born Michael (Kayne Legacy 2)

Poetry
Follow Me: Poetry from the Heart and Soul
The Courtship of the Vampyre

Sassy Vixen Publishing Anthologies
Sweet, Sultry, and Oh So Taboo
Season of Sun and Sin

www.ingramcontent.com/pod-product-compliance
Lightning Source LLC
Chambersburg PA
CBHW030508130626
46549CB00007B/2896